MR. RUSH

by Roger Hargreaves

Mr Rush was the fastest thing on two legs.

He used to rush hither and thither, and thither and hither, and back again, all the time.

And, of course, he was always in such a rush that he never ever finished anything properly.

One morning he woke up with a jump.

He'd only had time for three hours' sleep because he'd been rushing about for so long the day before.

"Oh dear," he cried, leaping out of bed. "I'm late!"

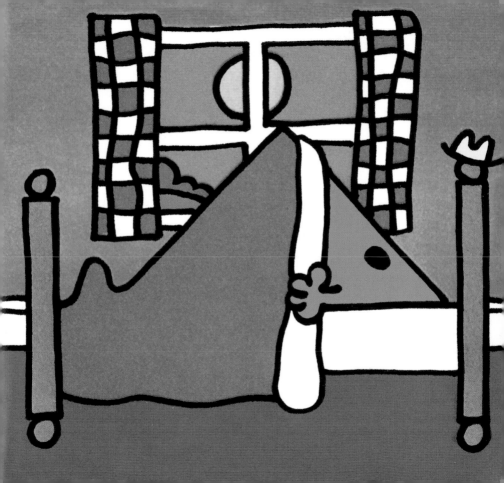

And he rushed into his bathroom, and washed (not very well as he was in such a hurry) and cleaned one tooth, and rushed downstairs – three at a time.

Mr Rush had a boiled egg and toast and a cup of tea for breakfast.

He boiled the egg for five seconds, and it tasted awful.

He toasted the bread for one second, and so it wasn't brown at all.

And, as he couldn't bear to wait for the kettle to boil, he made his tea with cold water.

Ugh!

What a horrid breakfast.

And, of course, he was in such a rush he only ate half of it.

Rush. Rush. Rush.

Silly fellow!

After his half a breakfast he rushed off again.

Out of his front door (leaving it open), down his garden path, out of his garden gate (leaving it open too), and off down the lane.

He passed Mr Happy.

"Hello," called Mr Happy. "Good morning, Mr Rush. Where are you off to?"

"Can't stop," cried Mr Rush. "I'm in much too much of a hurry!"

"I can see that," thought Mr Happy to himself as he watched Mr Rush disappear into the distance. "I wonder where he's going?"

Where Mr Rush was going was nowhere.

Fast!

As usual.

Mr Rush rushed around all morning, and then rushed home and had a quick bite to eat (a sandwich without bread), and then rushed off again.

And rushed around all afternoon!

That evening, he was reading a magazine (he never had time to read a book) when he saw an advertisement for a holiday.

"Ooo," he said. "I'd like that. Haven't had a holiday for ages."

But then his face fell.

"I can't go on holiday," he thought, "because I don't have any money."

And then he thought again.

And his face rose.

"I know," he thought, "I'll get a job."

And so, the following morning, he rushed off and got a job.

With a farmer.

Milking cows!

But of course he wasn't any good at that because, if there's one thing a cow can't stand, it's being rushed.

Especially when it's being milked!

So, Mr Rush rushed off and got himself another job.

Driving a bus!

But of course he wasn't any good at that because he was always in such a rush he never stopped at any of the bus stops!

And, if there's one thing people waiting at a bus stop don't like, it's when the bus doesn't stop for them.

So, Mr Rush rushed off and got himself another job.

As a waiter in a hotel!

But of course he wasn't any good at that because, no sooner had he served people a meal, and they'd taken one bite, than he whisked the plate away from under their noses.

And, if there's one thing hungry people can't stand, its having food whisked away from them.

Poor Mr Rush.

No job.

No money!

"Oh dear," he sighed to himself. "I'm never going to be able to go on holiday."

He looked very glum and gloomy.

But then an idea struck him.

An idea for a job for someone who rushes around all the time.

An ideal job for someone who was the fastest thing on two legs.

Do you know what that job was?

Would you like to know what that job was?

Postman!

Delivering express letters.

Mr Rush was so good at it, he delivered twice as many letters in half the time any postman had ever done it before.

Soon he had saved enough money for that holiday of his.

And so, the very next week, there was Mr Rush sitting on a beach in the hot sunshine under a palm tree on holiday.

"This is the life," he grinned.

And rushed off for a swim.

His fifteenth that day!

And then it was breakfast time!

Psychiatric Aspects of
Neurologic Diseases

Psychiatric Aspects
of Neurologic Diseases

Practical Approaches
to Patient Care

Edited by

Constantine G. Lyketsos, MD, MHS,
Peter V. Rabins, MD, MPH,
John R. Lipsey, MD, *and*
Phillip R. Slavney, MD

Department of Psychiatry and Behavioral Sciences
Johns Hopkins University School of Medicine

OXFORD
UNIVERSITY PRESS

2008

OXFORD
UNIVERSITY PRESS

Oxford University Press, Inc., publishes works that further
Oxford University's objective of excellence
in research, scholarship, and education.

Oxford   New York
Auckland   Cape Town   Dar es Salaam   Hong Kong   Karachi
Kuala Lumpur   Madrid   Melbourne   Mexico City   Nairobi
New Delhi   Shanghai   Taipei   Toronto

With offices in
Argentina   Austria   Brazil   Chile   Czech Republic   France   Greece
Guatemala   Hungary   Italy   Japan   Poland   Portugal   Singapore
South Korea   Switzerland   Thailand   Turkey   Ukraine   Vietnam

Copyright © 2008 by Oxford University Press, Inc.

Published by Oxford University Press, Inc.
198 Madison Avenue, New York, New York 10016

www.oup.com

Oxford is a registered trademark of Oxford University Press

The science of medicine is a rapidly changing field. New research and clinical experience
produces changes in treatment and drug therapy. The editors, contributors, and publisher of
this work have made every effort to provide accurate drug doses and medical information
in accordance with the standards accepted at the time of publication. However, because
human error or changes in the practice of medicine do occur, the editors, contributors,
and publisher cannot be held responsible for errors or for any consequences arising from the
use of information herein contained. Readers are encouraged to confirm the information
with other reliable sources, and are strongly advised to check the product information
sheet provided by the pharmaceutical company for each drug they plan to administer.
Ultimately, responsibility for a patient's care rests with the prescribing physician.

Library of Congress Cataloging-in-Publication Data
Psychiatric aspects of neurologic diseases : practical approaches to patient care / edited by
Constantine G. Lyketsos ... [et al.].
p. ; cm.
Includes bibliographical references and index.
ISBN-13: 978-0-19-530943-0
1. Nervous system—Diseases—Complications.   2. Nervous system—Diseases—Patients—
Care.   3. Psychological manifestations of general diseases.   4. Mental illness—Etiology.
5. Mental illness—Treatment.
[DNLM: 1. Nervous System Diseases—complications.   2. Mental Disorders—etiology.
3. Mental Disorders—therapy. WL 140 P9735 2008]   I. Lyketsos, Constantine G.
RC346.P82 2008
616.8'0475—dc22
2007024220

9 8 7 6 5 4 3 2 1
Printed in the United States of America
on acid-free paper